Winnie in the Sun

LAURA OWEN & KORKY PAUL

OXFORD
UNIVERSITY PRESS

Helping your child to read

Before they start

- ★ Read the back cover blurb with your child. Have they ever felt hot and bothered when the weather was too warm? How did it make them feel? How did they cool down?
- ★ How does your child think Winnie would feel if Wilbur disappeared? Why?

During reading

- ★ Let your child read at their own pace – don't worry if it's slow. Offer them plenty of help if they get stuck, and enjoy the story together.
- ★ Help them to work out words they don't know by saying each sound out loud and then blending them to say the word, e.g. *c-au-l-d-r-o-n, cauldron*.
- ★ If your child still struggles with a word, just tell them the word and move on.
- ★ Give them lots of praise for good reading!

After reading

- ★ Look at page 48 for some fun activities.

Contents

OXFORD
UNIVERSITY PRESS

Great Clarendon Street, Oxford OX2 6DP
Oxford University Press is a department of the University of Oxford.
It furthers the University's objective of excellence in research, scholarship,
and education by publishing worldwide. Oxford is a registered trade mark
of Oxford University Press in the UK and in certain other countries

Text © Oxford University Press
Illustrations © Korky Paul

The characters in this work are the original creation of Valerie Thomas
who retains copyright in the characters.

"Hot Cross Winnie" was first published in *Whizz-Bang Winnie,* 2008
"Winnie Digs Deep" was first published in *Winnie Goes Batty,* 2010

This edition published 2020

The moral rights of the author/illustrator have been asserted

Database right Oxford University Press (maker)

British Library Cataloguing in Publication Data

Data available

ISBN: 978-0-19-277376-0

3 5 7 9 10 8 6 4

OX27778202

Printed in China

Paper used in the production of this book is a natural,
recyclable product made from wood grown in sustainable forests.
The manufacturing process conforms to the environmental
regulations of the country of origin.

Hot Cross Winnie

One sunny day, Wilbur was lying in the shade.

Winnie's garden was as hot as a cauldron.

Winnie was wearing very dark sunglasses, so she didn't see him as she came along.

Trip!

"Meeoww-oww-oww!" said Wilbur.

"Oh, bats and beetles, Wilbur!" said
Winnie crossly.

"Meeow!" Wilbur was cross, too.

"Oh dear," said Winnie. "I'm a hot cross witch, and you're a hot cross cat. We need to cool down!"

Winnie waved her wand. "**Abracadabra!**"

At once, there was a giant watering can.

It tipped lovely cold water all over them.

"Yippee!" said Winnie, dancing in

the shower.

But Wilbur was **not** happy. "**Hissss!**"

"I'm sorry, Wilbur!" said Winnie. "I forgot cats don't like water!"

She made the watering can vanish, and magicked up a sunhat and sunglasses.

But Wilbur was still cross.

"A joke will cheer you up!" said Winnie.

"What's brown and sticky and sounds like a bell?"

Wilbur ignored her.

"Dung!" said Winnie. "Dung's brown and sticky, and 'dung' is the sound a big bell makes. Get it?"

But Wilbur said nothing.

"I know!" said Winnie. "I'll buy you a present, Wilbur. That's bound to cheer you up!"

So Winnie and Wilbur got on the broomstick and flew to the shops.

Winnie parked her broom outside a shop.

"Stay in the broom basket, Wilbur," she said. "You can't come in the shop, or it will spoil the surprise."

As Winnie stepped into the shop, a draught of cool, smelly air blew around her. "Oooh!" she said. "That's a nice cold wind!"

But outside, Wilbur was still hot.

While Winnie was in the shop, a little girl called Clara came past. She saw Wilbur.

"Nice Pussykins!" she said. "Come with me!"

And she carried Wilbur all the way back to her house.

It was nice and cool in Clara's house.

Wilbur had a bowl of cat food. Clara and her sisters made a big fuss of him.

Wilbur purred so loudly his whiskers sparkled.

zzzzzzzing!

When Winnie came out of the shop, she got on the broom. She thought Wilbur was hiding in the basket.

"Are you still sulking, Wilbur?" she said. "Wait till you see your present!"

Winnie flew home as fast as she could.

But when she jumped off the broom and

looked for Wilbur she got a terrible shock!

The basket was empty.

Winnie went back to the shop to find him.

"Wilbur!" Winnie shouted. "Where are you!"

"That black cat?" asked a boy who worked in the shop. "Clara took him to her house. They went that way!"

"**Abracadabra!**" Winnie magicked herself to Clara's house.

At once she spotted Wilbur.

"Don't worry, Wilbur," shouted Winnie. "I've come to take you home."

"No!" said Clara. "Pussykins is going to live with me for ever!"

"But he's MY friend!" said Winnie. "Look, I've brought him a present!"

Clara and her sisters ripped open the present and found . . .

. . . an ice cream maker!

"We'll make lovely cool maggot ice creams, Wilbur!" said Winnie.

But Clara's mum made strawberry ice cream cones. Soon the girls had forgotten all about Wilbur.

"Quick, let's go home!" whispered Winnie.

They left the ice cream maker behind and

hopped on to the broomstick.

At home, Winnie and Wilbur found a nice shady spot by the pond.

"This is better!" said Winnie. "I've got another joke for you, Wilbur. What's brown and sticky?"

"Meeow," grinned Wilbur. He pointed to the fishing rod in Winnie's hand.

"That's right!" said Winnie. "A stick!"

Winnie Digs Deep

"Phew, Wilbur!" said Winnie. "I'm as hot as a hot dog with ten hot water bottles!"

She poured a jug of water over her head. The water turned to steam.

HISSSSS!

"Meeow," said Wilbur. He was hot, too.

"Let's go to the museum," said Winnie. "It's always nice and cool there."

Winnie was right. It was lovely and cool in the museum.

"**Ahhh!**" said Winnie loudly. "That's better!"

"**Ssssh!**" said the man in charge of the museum.

Then Winnie spotted a massive dinosaur skeleton.

"**Aaaargh!**" she yelled, even louder.

"Meeeow!" said Wilbur.

"I'm sorry, madam," said the museum man.

"We don't allow animals here. You'll have to take him home."

"That's a silly rule!" said Winnie crossly.

On the way out, Winnie saw cracked pots and dirty coins on the museum shelves.

"Let's dig up some bones and treasure in the garden, Wilbur," she said. "We can have our own museum!"

Back home, Wilbur got a spade. Then Winnie had a good idea. "**Abracadabra!**" She magicked up a metal detector.

"This will help us find a good place to dig, Wilbur," she said.

Suddenly, the metal detector made a noise. **Buzz!**

"Dig here, Wilbur," said Winnie.

Wilbur dug, dug, dug, in the hot sun. **Buzz! Buzz!** went the detector.

He found some junk, but no dinosaur bones.

And no treasure.

"Blithering beetles, Wilbur!" said Winnie. "That's just a lot of rusty rubbish!"

"Meeow!" said Wilbur, crossly.

"We need some help," said Winnie. "Go and get Jerry and Scruff, Wilbur."

Jerry was the giant who lived next door
and Scruff was his dog.
They dug an *enormous* hole!

It was hot work!

Winnie went in to fetch a jug of wiggly worm squash.

"Er, no thank you!" said Jerry, and he carried
on digging.

Soon, the hole was so big that you could hardly

see Jerry!

"Have you found anything good yet?"

asked Winnie.

"What about this?" said Jerry. He handed Winnie a shiny round metal thing.

"Oh!" said Winnie. "That's just my old saucepan!"

Jerry went on digging. The sun went on shining. Everyone got hotter and hotter.

At last Jerry held up something wriggly.

"Yummy!" said Winnie. "A new kind of bug!

Are there any more, Jerry?"

"There are lots of bugs down here!" said Jerry.

So Winnie went to the bottom of the hole.

She filled a big bucket with bugs.

"One more dig for luck," said

Jerry. Suddenly . . .

Jerry's spade made a hole in a water pipe.

Sploosh! Whoosh!

Soon, the hole was full of water.

Jerry swam up to the top. "Lovely!" he said.

"Ruff!" agreed Scruff.

"We've got our own swimming pool!"

said Winnie. "**Abracadabra!**"

She magicked up a water slide.

**wheee-
splosh!**

wheee-splosh!-yap!

went Scruff.

wheee-splosh!-
meeow!

went Wilbur.

45

Everyone whizzed down the slide.

Just then, the man from the museum came past.

"What a pile of junk!" he said. "I'd never put that rubbish in my museum!"

"We don't care, do we?" said Winnie. "Anyway, good friends are the best sort of treasure there is!"

The four friends agreed, then jumped into the water.

wheee-splosh!

After reading activities

Talk about the stories

Ask your child the following questions. Encourage them to talk about their answers.

1) In "Hot Cross Winnie", where does Wilbur disappear to?

2) In "Hot Cross Winnie", how do you think Winnie and Wilbur feel at the end, and why?

3) In "Winnie Digs Deep", do you agree with Winnie that friends are the best sort of treasure?

1) Clara's house; 2) Open question – child's own opinion; 3) Open question – child's own opinion.

Try this!

Imagine you dug a deep hole and found some treasure. What would the treasure be like? Draw it!